THE SPIRIT OF KRAMPUS

Kate Danley

Illustrated by

Abigail Larson

THE SPIRIT OF KRAMPUS

The wind howled down the street and swept the dry, fallen leaves through the gutter. The town's single stoplight flashed yellow for the cars that would never come. With no one left to run the power plants, the city's one time investment in utility solar panels now provided the only glimpses of electricity.

A few houses were lit with flickering candlelight, their shade-drawn windows creating the false warmth of home and hearth against a cold afternoon sky.

Two boys walked down the street, their breath making white clouds with every exhalation.

"Santa coming tonight, Bo?" asked the younger one. He had a shock of sandy brown hair and a spray of freckles across his chapped nose. He used his sleeve to wipe away a stream of snot as he looked up at his big brother, his eyes filled with adoration and hero worship. When their parents went mad, when he and Bo were placed in that foster home, when they had to run away, Bo was the one who took care of them. Bo was the one who made sure they were okay.

"No such thing as Santa Claus, Skip," Bo replied, shoving his hands deeper into his pockets. Bo's hair was darker and curlier than Skip's and his face was hard in a way that a kid's shouldn't be at thirteen. "Nuthin' but another night."

"But I remember this story..." Skip began.

"Nuthin' but a story. Don't let anybody tell you different."

Skip fell silent and trudged along beside his brother, his eight-year old legs going double time to match Bo's strides. He looked up at the glowing windows and whispered, "Maybe there's some nice ones inside. Maybe these ones have some food or something..."

"You know they're nuthin' but traps."

"But maybe it's different here."

Bo grabbed Skip's arm. "You've seen what they do. If you ever go up there..."

At that moment, a curtain parted and then closed again. The door opened and a woman stepped out onto her porch. She waved a hand at them and shouted, "Hello! Hello there!"

"Keep walking," Bo hissed at his brother.

"You boys doing okay? Brrr! It's so cold out here! Why don't you come in and warm yourself a spell?"

Skip slowed down, his heart filled with secret longing. The woman's dress was red and polka-dot, just like the pictures in that book about Santa Claus. Sure, her face was dirty and her curly hair looked kind of like it hadn't really been brushed, but she was holding a plate of cookies that were sparkly and green with squiggly white decorations.

"Aren't you hungry? Why don't you come on up and have a cookie!" she called. "They're fresh out of the oven! Made them special for Christmas Eve!"

"Bo, she has cookies..." said Skip.

Bo shook his head and warned, "She's lying. She wants to put you in her oven. Keep walking."

Skip trotted to catch up with his brother.

"Those cookies'll turn to ash in your mouth and into worms and slugs. They'll make you sick and you'll fall under her spell," Bo continued, making sure that Skip was listening. "You gotta promise me, Skip. You gotta promise me that if I'm ever not around you'll never talk to people like her. Don't talk to her. Don't look at her. You can't trust the grownups. Not anymore."

They walked on in silence as the woman called out after them, pleading for them to come back.

Skip tried to remember what it was like before they started looking for other kids. The memories were fading. Everyday seemed like the one before - just putting one foot in front of the other. They slept in the woods and got food wherever they could find it - in empty restaurants, abandoned grocery stores, overgrown gardens... At first, there were a lot of boys and girls their age, but one after another, they went into those houses with the friendly looking grownups and none of them ever came out again.

From far behind, there was a scream like a roaring lion who ran her nails across glass.

"Told you she was no good," said Bo.

Skip gulped. "Thanks, Bo."

He tripped a little as he looked back wistfully.

"Tell me a story, Bo..." Skip asked.

Bo blew out his breath and watched the smoke rise like a cloud. "What do you want a story about?"

"Tell me the story about how the grownups used to be different."

"Again?"

"It's my favorite!" Skip begged.

Bo looked like he was thinking it over, but Skip knew better. He knew his brother would tell him the story. He liked to remember as much as Skip liked to hear about it.

"Come on..."

Bo dragged out the suspense. It was a game, but the only game they had left.

"Okay, but this is the last time," said Bo, though Skip knew that wasn't true.

"The last time, I promise," said Skip, though they knew that wasn't true, either.

"Once upon a time..."

"Which was just last Christmas!"

"Right, last Christmas. Once upon a time, which was about a year ago, the grown-ups were nice. They were like us, only bigger. They laughed and told jokes and kids didn't have to worry about food or being eaten or nuthin'."

"And then what happened?"

"Am I telling the story or not?"

"Sorry, Bo."

"Okay, so on Christmas Eve, something happened."

"What happened?"

"It was like they all went crazy. They stopped worrying about being good and it was like all the sudden all they cared about was who could be the meanest. And then something snapped and kids like you and me, they started disappearing. Just gone. We used to go to school then, remember?"

"I forget.... what was that like?"

Bo shrugged. "It was nice. They gave you juice and read you stories and sometimes you could draw pictures and stuff."

"You used to like drawing pictures?"

"Yah. I liked it a lot."

"We can still draw pictures," said Skip.

"With what?"

"Maybe if we ever find some markers..."

Bo picked up a rock and saw how far he could throw it. "Sure, Skip. If we ever get some markers that work, we'll draw all day."

"If there was such thing as Santa, we could ask him to bring us some markers."

"Ain't no such thing as Santa."

"I know."

Bo continued his story, "So pretty soon the grown-ups weren't nice anymore and it's like what you see in that house. They seem like they care, but any kid who goes in disappears. You can't trust 'em."

Skip nodded.

"But now you and me are a team. As long as we stay to the middle of the road, they can't come out and get us. As long as you don't ever go inside, we're safe."

Skip looked along the deserted street. "You figure we're the last kids on earth?"

"Yeah," replied Bo. "I ain't never seen anyone like us for a long time."

"And we can't ever let the grownups get us."

"Do you remember what'll happen if they get us?"

"They'll put us in a bag and beat us with a stick and then take us home and eat us for supper."

Bo nodded and put his arm around Skip. He gave him a little hug. "But I'll never let that happened."

The wind began to blow.

"Never let what happen?" asked a voice.

Skip and Bo looked over. In one of the yards, far off the porch and away from the house, was a strange creature. He looked almost like a goat, except he walked on two legs. He was as tall as a grownup, but he was covered in white fur with black tips. He had horns upon his head, his face was long, and his teeth were sharp. Over his shoulder, he carried a black sack and in his hand he carried a bundle of golden switches.

"Don't pay him no mind, Skip," said Bo. "Just keep on walking. He can't get us."

The creature gave him a knowing look and then jumped over the fence, bounded across the sidewalk, and landed in the middle of the road right in front of them.

Bo put his hand on Skip's shoulder and they both froze. Skip knew his big brother could take care of them. He knew his brother would never be scared, so he stood quiet, ready to run whenever Bo told him.

"I hear you have been very naughty," said the creature.

"Not us," said Bo.

The creature tilted his head and his mouth broke into something that appeared to be a smile. Bo did not smile back.

"I heard that nice grownup tell you to come in her house and you disobeyed," he said to Bo. "You even forced that child... I believe you called him 'Skip'... that boy who stands beside you... you forced him to disobey her. And now you are lying to me about being good. I find you very, very naughty, indeed."

Bo stuck out his chin. "I'm almost a man. I don't follow grown up rules like some kid."

The creature shook his head. "If you were a man, you would be indoors, unable to come out except for Christmas Eve. But here you are. You must be even naughtier then I thought."

Bo turned to his brother, his eyes never leaving the creature. "Run..."

The creature threw his bag to the ground and opened up the mouth. The sound that emerged was a roar. "GET IN MY SACK, YOU NAUGHTY BOY!"

A great vortex erupted from inside. It moved like a tornado and wrapped around Bo's body, yanking him towards the bag. Skip threw his arms around his brother and hung on, even as Bo's feet lifted from the ground.

"Go get help, Skip!" Bo shouted, the wind carrying away his words.

Bo began to slip and Skip grabbed to catch his arms, and then clutched at his hands as he continued to slide.

"I won't let you go!" Skip cried, choking as tears closed his throat.

Bo shook his head, showing fear for the first time Skip had ever seen, and screamed, "Get help! RUN!"

And Bo was torn away.

In an instant, he was sucked into the bag.

Skip did not look back as he ran, ran and wondered

where in the world he could go to get help when he was all alone in the world.

The home was burrowed into the side of an overgrown gulch. It looked different than any other building he had ever seen. Skip would have raced right by if it wasn't for the red and white striped pole standing like a marker by the road. Next to the pole was a narrow dirt path leading down the steep gully, through a sea of fern and ivy, to a small, round front door.

Skip slowed to a stop. Hesitantly, he wandered back, wondering if this different looking house might have a different sort of person living inside. Bo would have known what to do, he thought, Bo would have known if it was safe.

Skip rested his hand upon the pole. It seemed to warm against his palm. It made him feel a little better, kind of like when Bo would put his arms around his shoulders and tell him he was brave.

He needed to be brave for Bo, he decided.

He forced one foot forward. And then the other. And then another until he was walking down to the building, sliding a little on the slope as he went. He raced to the door before he could change his mind and pounded his fists upon it in time to the pounding of his heart.

A little pointed hat and little pointed ears appeared in the window, then a curly mop of red hair and a small set of beady eyes. Those eyes got bigger when they saw who was standing outside. He disappeared and the door opened to reveal a pie-faced man not even as tall as Skip's shoulder. He wore red tights and a red tunic with green tips on all the edges.

"Are you naughty or nice?" the little man squeaked.

"Nice...?" said Skip.

"You sure?"

Skip nodded hesitantly.

"Come in!" he waved.

Skip didn't move. Instead he asked, "Are you a grown up?"

"No, of course not!" said the little man. "Now get inside before anyone sees you."

"Please, sir... my brother..." said Skip, pointing back to where his brother was taken.

The little man pulled him over the threshold, panic in his voice. "We'll talk inside."

The house seemed much bigger than the hill. Everything was carved out of honey-colored wood.

Big fluffy couches and chairs covered in red and green plaid sat next to a crackling fire in the fireplace. The air smelled of something that made Skip's mouth water.

"You must be hungry," said the little man, darting around the room like a bird. He held up a plate. "Here, would you like a cookie?"

The plate was filled with gingerbread men decorated with green and white frosting. Skip's breath caught in his throat and wildly he looked for a way out.

"Wait! Wait!" said the man, putting down the tray and holding up his hands in peace. "I forgot. I forgot that is how they try to lure you in. I'm sorry! There's not many of you left and I forgot myself! It used to be that you could offer a child a cookie and it was a kindness..."

The man stopped himself and looked like he was trying to gather his thoughts.

"My name is Herbie." The little man pointed at himself. "I'm an elf."

Skip gulped. "My brother Bo says there's no such thing as elves."

"Oh my," said Herbie, distraught. He sat down on a stool by the fire as if someone had punched him in the stomach. "No such thing as elves... I wonder what I am? No wonder everything when so wrong... to have been lied to... even by my own mother! She said I was an elf. And now to learn that your brother thinks even she was deceiving me..."

"Maybe my brother was wrong," offered Skip, feeling bad.

"Oh, I'm sure he knows the world much better than me. You believe him. Even more than what you see in front of your very eyes. That must mean I am all mixed up." Herbie looked up. "What's your name?"

"Skip."

"And since I am so wrong about so many things, what are you?"

Skip shifted awkwardly. "I'm a boy. Just a... boy."

"Oh!" said Herbie. "I used to build toys for good boys. And good girls, too. Only, there aren't many children left. So now I don't."

Skip pointed to the door, begging. "Herbie, my brother is in trouble."

"Step away from the window where terrible things might be watching!" said Herbie, grabbing Skip and hauling him over to the couch.

He pushed Skip into the cushions and tucked a fuzzy blanket around his legs. Herbie sat back on his stool and rested his chin on his hands. "Now, tell me what kind of trouble."

Skip didn't know what to make of the elf. He seemed absentminded and blinked too much, but he also seemed kind. Skip stroked the blanket. He didn't have anyone else to turn to. "There was a big shaggy creature with horns and he sucked my brother up and put him in his sack."

Herbie became very still. He shook his head with a faraway look and whispered, "Krampus."

"What's 'Krampus'?"

"Krampus is a 'who', not a 'what'," said Herbie. "And he's been out of control ever since Santa disappeared."

"Santa disappeared?" asked Skip. "But my brother says Santa doesn't—"

Herbie gave him a horrified look. Skip bit back his words. Instead he asked, "How?"

Herbie picked up a cookie, chewing as he remembered. "I was away from the North Pole. I was here, to keep track of how the boys and girls were behaving, when Santa disappeared... when I became stranded... if Santa were still alive, he would have come to get me... I am sure... instead, I'm here..."

Herbie's voice trailed off and for a minute, Skip though the elf might cry, but then he continued, "With no one to keep the naughty and nice list, I heard Krampus took it upon himself decide who was which. It was right about the same time that all the grown-ups went plum crazy. Seemed like they were almost working to make their children misbehave, working to get them on that naughty list. And then they started putting kids in bags, any kids they could find. It was like the spirit of Christmas got replaced by the spirit of Krampus."

"Is that what Krampus does?" asked Skip.

"Back in the day, he used to ride with St. Nicholas... That's what people used to call Santa... St. Nicholas would give gifts to the good boys and girls. But if you were wicked, Krampus would come and put you in his sack and beat you with his sticks and then take you home to eat for his Christmas dinner."

Skip whispered, "Is he going to eat Bo?"

Herbie didn't answer.

"Please, Herbie," he begged, "If Krampus got my brother..."

"If Krampus got your brother, your brother is in terrible danger," said Herbie.

"Will you help me get him back?" asked Skip.

Herbie seemed very small at that moment, even smaller and more scared that Skip felt. "There's no getting him back. I know Krampus. I saw him every Christmas. It is best to forget about your brother and move on with your life."

Skip wanted Herbie to fix everything. He wanted someone to come along and make it all better. He wanted to be walking along the road with his big brother and for everyone to stay in their yards.

But that wasn't real. It was just wishes.

Skip looked at the plate of cookies, at the kindness the little elf had tried to extend to him.

His brother had been wrong about elves, he thought. Maybe he was wrong about Christmas, too.

"What if saving my brother is my Christmas wish?" asked Skip.

"There is no one who can make your wish come true anymore," said Herbie. "No one can stop Krampus except Santa and he's gone."

Herbie stopped himself.   He became thoughtful. "But maybe..."

"What?"

Herbie picked up another cookie and bit it with fast little nibbles as the idea formed. "If you could get to the North Pole and find Santa..."

"How?"

"You'd first have to find the workshop. It has a pole in front of it that looks like mine. The few of us elves who are still around have been putting out poles like that so we can keep track of one another." Herbie looked at Skip, rubbing his chin with his finger. "Kind of funny that you were able to see it."

Herbie got up from the couch and walked over to a closet. He opened it up. Inside were piles of metal and plastic. He spoke faster and faster as he set aside bits and pieces. "Now, to get to the North Pole, you're going to need one of Santa's flying reindeer, and I'm afraid I don't have one of those. If I had a reindeer, I wouldn't be here. I would be in the North Pole."

Skip stood and walked over to Herbie. "Can I get one somewhere?"

"Yes! Oh my, yes!" said Herbie. There was a mad look in his eyes. "We'll have to find you a flying reindeer. It is your Christmas wish! If there is one around, they'll be in the woods. There are woods at the far end of town. I can't go there. I have to stay here in case Santa comes for me. But you can! You can go! Only it's almost Christmas Eve and pretty soon those grownups are going to be able to get out of their yards..."

Skip looked at the pile of materials Herbie was gathering up. "Are you making something?"

"You'll need a disguise. Something to fool the grownups just long enough for you to slip through." Herbie grinned before diving back into the closet. "If there's any Christmas magic left, I will make sure you get your wish."

They peeked out from the ditch that hid Herbie's house. There were rows of houses between them and the woods and the sun was starting to set. Skip began shaking.

"You have to act like a toy!" Herbie whispered.

All about them, the grown-ups had left their houses and were milling around their front yards. They were looking at each other with wicked smiles, gleefully clasping their hands together like three year olds about to get a glorious surprise. At their feet were wiggling black sacks, which they kicked from time to time.

"Happy Christmas!" the wished one another.

"Happy Christmas!" they said, grasping one another's hand.

"No magic like Christmas magic!"

"To finally be able to leave! To be able to walk around the world for one night!"

"A glorious thing!"

"I brought my sack full of children! I brought him so

many, maybe he'll let me have two nights out!"

"I've got so many, maybe he'll let me have three!"

All along the street, anxious hands gripped the fence posts waiting for the sun to dip behind the mountains and the first star to light the sky.

"Be really careful around them," whispered Herbie. "Make sure to get to the woods before the sun sets. Go now before they can get out of their yards."

Skip nodded, looking down at himself. Herbie had taken bits of metal and plastic and had bent them around Skip's arms and legs until he looked like a life-sized tin soldier with a wind up key in his back. "You sure this is going to fool them?"

"Of course!" said Herbie, his innocent eyes shining with pride.

"Thank you for helping me," said Skip. He reached over and grabbed him up in a hug.

"Careful!" said Herbie, backing off to put Skip's outfit back in place. "Now remember, you only have until the Christmas feast at midnight. That's what they've been capturing all the children for. After that, there's no saving your brother or anyone else."

Skip nodded and crawled up to the street. He squared his little shoulders and tried to make his eyes appear as blank as a wind-up doll.

"Merry Christmas, Skip!"

Skip took his first step down the middle of the road.

Slowly, he marched towards the woods, matching his pace to the clockwork rhythm, Be brave for Bo... be brave for Bo...

"Oh look!" cried a grownup man in a grey suit from a house half way down the block. "A Christmas parade!"

Be brave for Bo...be brave for Bo...

Skip felt all eyes upon him. He felt them staring. He tried to keep his eyes blank, but a cold gust of wind was blowing. And he blinked.

"He blinked..." said a woman.

"Do you think it is one of those dolls with the sleepy eyes?"

"No, they only close if you lay them on their back..."

"I don't think that's a toy..." said another.

"I think it's a child trying to fool us!" shouted another.

Skip looked to the side fearfully and all the men and women from every house started shaking their gates and throwing themselves against their fences like wild beasts. "IT'S A CHILD! A LYING CHILD! A NAUGHTY CHILD WHO SHOULD BE PUT IN A SACK!"

From far away, Skip heard Herbie shout, "I'm sorry! I'm sorry Skip! This was not a good plan!"

Skip began to run. He ran as fast as his little legs could carry him. His costume clanked with every step, the hard, jointed edges that Herbie had so lovingly fitted knocking against one another as he tore off down the road.

He neared the edge of the forest just as the sun dipped

behind the trees. He did not look back as he heard every gate on the street opened in one movement and the sound of the grownups racing after him with their bags in their hands.

He hit the tree line as the light faded into twilight, as snow began to fall from the sky. His breath came in ragged gasps and his lungs felt as if they were on fire. He could hear the grownups' high heeled shoes and slick loafers crunching and sliding on the pine needles and hidden branches behind him.

He came to an embankment and slid down, hoping the people would think he had stayed on the path.

He ran on, looking for someplace, anyplace to hide.

"Come here you naughty little boy! Running is so disobedient. I have a sack waiting for you to punish you for your sins!" came the cry.

Skip ducked behind a tree and waited, hoping they would pass by, hoping they could not hear his panting breath.

Bo would have known what to do, he thought. Bo would have gotten them someplace safe.

But Bo was not here.

Just then, Skip thought he heard the crack of a twig. He stood completely still, like a deer who had caught the smell of a wolf.

"AH! I've got you!"

A brown haired man in ragged clothes jumped around

the tree. He reached out and missed Skip by inches. Skip dodged and wove, running in between one tree and the next, trying to escape the man's hands and outstretched bag.

"There he is!" came a distant voice.

Skip glanced up and saw the entire town start to make its way down the embankment.

"Get in my bag!"

"No, get in MY bag!"

"I said to get in my bag!" they called out to him.

Skip took off, not sure where he was going. Despite the bite to the air, sweat poured down his face and dripped down his back.

He tripped, and someone tried to grab his ankle. He kicked and hit the grownup square in the teeth. Face bleeding, the man cried, "You are very naughty indeed! Get in my sack!"

Skip scrambled to his feet and ran some more.

And then, suddenly, he slid to a halt. Before him was an overhang which dropped a hundred feet to a small froze brook below. There was nowhere to run, nowhere to escape. Nothing left to do but to be brave and fight. Skip adjusted the soldier costume as it bit into his ribs and turned to face the horde of maddened parents slowly stalked towards him chanting, "Get in my sack... get in my sack..."

But then there was a sound. It was the sound of

jingling. It was distant at first, but then it came closer. It was a sound that caused everyone to stop and look.

And at that moment, a reindeer with golden antlers bounced over the heads of the crowd. She wore a red saddle and a halter covered in large brass bells.

The reindeer seemed not to care who she trampled to get to the boy. She tore through the crowd, striking anyone who tried to interfere with her silver hooves. Desperately, Skip and the deer raced towards each other. The deer bent down and the moment Skip touched her, he felt as light as a feather. He flew over the reindeer, twisting and turning, and landed in her saddle.

The creature lowered her head at the crowd, as if daring them to step forward and attack her charge.

"Let's get out of here," whispered Skip.

As if waiting for this command, the reindeer leapt and took off into the sky. Skip clung to her neck and squeezed his eyes shut, hoping that it was just a dream.

But it was not. The moment he opened his eyes, the world was as real as it was a moment before, the land racing fast below him as they sailed across the sky.

"Thank you for saving me," he whispered.

The reindeer threw back her head and nodded, as if thanking him, too.

It seemed like hours later, and at the same time an instant, when they finally reached a flat cold expanse of glaciers and snow. There was a white barber shop pole with red stripes, almost like the one that Herbie had in front of his house, except this one was larger and stood at the mouth of a giant cave.

The reindeer landed and walked forward, her hooves crunching the ground with each step. As she passed the cave's entrance, a curtain of ice closed behind them, and a wall of ice opened in front.

The full moon shone through the frozen roof and dimly lit the room before them. It looked like it might have once been a workshop of sorts, a place where toys were made, but now the brightly colored playthings lay on the ground, smashed and destroyed, and there was no sign of the workers.

The reindeer stopped by a large lever built into the wall. Skip leaned over, grabbed the brass handle, and pulled it down. A deep hum filled the room and, one-by-one, the lights overhead flickered and came to life.

The destruction was terrible. There were holes in the walls where heavy things had been thrown, every conveyor belt had been ripped off its rollers, workstations had been tipped over and all the chairs were broken into splinters.

"What happened?" asked Skip.

He got off the reindeer and began walking carefully through the wreckage. The reindeer followed behind.

"There must have been a battle," he said as he looked a doll whose head had been crushed. His voice echoed through the building.

"Hello?" Skip called. "Santa?"

There was no response. The reindeer gazed off towards a separate room.

The double doors had been torn off their hinges and the maw of the arched entry stood waiting. Skip made his way around the bits of plastic, metal, and glass and went in.

It was a stable, each stall busted apart from the inside. Skip turned to the reindeer and asked, "Did you have to break out?"

The reindeer nodded her head. Skip pointed to the name plates over each of the nine stalls. "Which one were you?"

The reindeer delicately picked her way over to one of the center stalls.

"Dasher?" asked Skip. "Are you Dasher?"

Once again, the reindeer nodded.

Skip walked over and placed his hand upon the reindeer's nose. "It is nice to meet you, Dasher."

Dasher let out a chuff of warm air and nudged his shoulder. Skip continued on through room after wrecked room - candy rooms, chocolate rooms, toy rooms and playgrounds - until he found himself in a large storage area. There were open filing cabinets from floor to ceiling in every direction he turned. On one side of the aisle, the empty drawers said "Nice." Upon the drawers on the other side, they all said "Naughty." Burned pages covered the room, the contents now nothing more than flaky, black shards.

"This was where Santa kept the naughty and nice list?" asked Skip, running his hand along the drawers. "How did it all catch on fire?"

Dasher gave him a look, as if asking him to think deeper.

"Unless someone set it on fire..."

Dasher flung her head up and down.

"But why would anyone do that?"

Dasher didn't seem to have an answer to this question.

Skip pushed away the ash with his feet, looking for any signs or clues. Row after row he searched until in the far corner, he saw a flash of white. The paper was almost completely hidden. But he saw it. Skip bent over and brushed away the soot. Written on the page were three little words: "Skip Albreight – Nice."

It was strange that such a simple piece of paper would make him feel so funny inside. It made him remember a happy time before his parents went crazy, back before foster care, and before he and Bo ran away...

Just then, a cabinet moved. Behind it was a little door. It would have been too big for a grown up to get through. The only people small enough to walk inside would be an elf... or a small boy.

Skip grabbed the paper and tucked it into his pocket. He got down on his hands and knees. He crawled through and found himself in a low ceilinged room. In the center, a red coat with white trim waited upon a dress form.

A large, green velvet sack hung from a hook. And in between the two was a table with a yellowed piece of parchment paper and a quill.

Skip walked over to the parchment. The curly writing was hard for him to read, but slowly, he sounded it out:

Welcome young traveler! If you are here, it is because a terrible event has occurred. The world is in peril. Take the sack and the coat. When the time is right, you will know what to do. You may have thought you were all alone, but you are not. No one can stop the spirit of Christmas.

Signed,
Santa Claus

Skip looked at the coat. He touched the soft, fur lined cuffs and rough, velvet sleeve. Reverently, he took it down and slipped into it. It was warm and felt like a hug. It smelled good, like vanilla and cinnamon. It was too big for him, but if he rolled up the arms and belted the waist tightly with the black belt, it didn't fall off. He lifted the bag. It seemed light and slung comfortably across his back.

Just then, the piece of paper with his name on it fluttered out of his pocket and fell to the floor. He stood there, dressed in Santa's clothes, staring at the last remaining page of the "Naughty & Nice" list. He picked it up and placed it on the table.

It seemed like there should be more names on that paper, he thought to himself. He took the quill from the inkwell, which dropped thick black blobs all over the page, but he didn't know what to write. There were so many people in the world and so many people who were missing. He didn't know who was good or bad. It seemed too big and too hard.

But then thought of his brother. Of the way that he was always there for him, the way Bo looked out for him and kept him safe. In his best handwriting, he scrawled, "Bo Albreight – Nice."

But then he thought about it a little more. He knew one more name that belonged on his list. He flipped over the paper to the blank side, dipped the quill in more ink, and wrote: "Krampus – Naughty."

There was still something wrong. He looked at the page and then looked at it twice. And then he remembered. By all three names, he placed two checkmarks.

Finally, it felt done.

Dasher's nose snuffed the doorway and Skip turned around.

"I'll be just a minute," he called.

He patted the list as he thought about his brother and thought about Krampus, and as he thought about how the whole world was being ruined.

His brother always told him to be brave.

Skip turned to the door and said, "Dasher, we have to go back."

Dasher landed behind an old school house and Skip pulled himself down from her back. Tiptoeing, he rounded the corner.

All the grownups were in the town square. The gazebo was on fire and the blaze was so big, it looked like it could burn for a whole month without ever going out.

The grownups laughed and danced, drank and cursed, breaking their bottles on the ground whenever they needed to punch someone.

A great big spit was built over the fire, and Skip didn't want to even think about what they were planning on using it for.

There was a squat, white building on the far side guarded by two angry looking adults. A man with a wiggling sack full of children walked up to the door. They opened it for him and he threw the bag inside.

"That must be where all the kids are," whispered Skip. "But how are we ever going to get inside?"

Dasher nuzzled Skip's shoulder.

"Not now, Dasher. I'm thinkin'."

Dasher nipped him this time.

"What?" asked Skip, turning around. "You have an idea?"

Dasher turned her head and touched her nose to the saddle.

"You want me to get on your back?" Skip asked.

Dasher nodded her head.

"Okay, but this had better be good," said Skip, climbing aboard.

Dasher took off into the sky, flying around the outskirts of town so that no one would see them. Everything outside the square was empty and dark. Her bells rang softly, rhythmically, and Skip began humming the memory of a long forgotten song. "Up on the roof top reindeer pause...Out jumps good old Santa Claus..."

Dasher landed delicately on the flat roof the white building.

Skip dismounted and threw Santa's bag over his shoulder. He smoothed Dasher's coat and stroked her face. Dasher looked at him with her big, soulful eyes and she pressed her nose against his cheek.

"Thank you, Dasher," he whispered.

He crept to the edge of the eaves and looked down. The adults were still reveling and didn't seem to have noticed them. Skip shrunk back

"Down through the chimney with lots of toys..." Skip murmured as he looked around. Then he got an idea. "Maybe this place has a chimney..."

Dasher tiptoed behind him and nudged him towards the spinning attic vents. Skip shook his head. "That is not going to work."

But Dasher pushed him again.

He looked at them. There was no way he could fit through. They were nothing but slits of metal turning quickly in the wind. If he were the wind, he thought, he could blow in no problem. He held Santa's bag tightly and thought about it some more.

If only he were the wind...

He felt a tingling in his toes. It felt like someone was tickling him, and working their way up from his feet to the top of his head. He couldn't help but giggle. A cold breeze swept around him and gave him a hug. And then suddenly, he was the wind. He blew himself over to the air ducts and danced inside. He flowed through the walls and then fell out into a room filled with wriggling bags, bags heavy with children.

Skip patted his body. He was solid once again. He ran over to the first bag and undid the knot.

A little girl's freckled face peeked out at him as he pulled back the flaps.

"Santa?" she asked.

"I'm not Santa. I'm looking for my brother Bo," he said

and moved to the next bag.

"Wait!" she called, wriggling and trying to free herself. "Help me!"

In one of the bags was his brother. He knew it. And he needed to get to his brother before the midnight bells tolled.

"Help me Santa!" she cried.

The other sacks stopped moving as the children inside listened. Skip could hear them whispering through the canvas to one another, "Santa is here?"

They started calling softly, "Help me, Santa! Help!"

"I'm not Santa!" he protested.

Skip stood in the middle of the room, their pleas like murmuring waves lapping at his ankles.

Bo always looked out for him, Skip thought. Bo would have known what to do.

But Bo wasn't there to tell him. He had to look into his own heart.

And in that moment, Skip knew.

Whether he found his brother or not, it was his turn to be someone else's Bo.

He ran back to the bag. The little girl's hands and feet had been bound.

"What's your name?" Skip asked as he worked on the knots.

"Molly."

The ropes finally loosened. "You're free, Molly.

Are you okay?"

She nodded and stood up. She didn't run away. Instead, she turned to Skip and said, "I'll help you, Santa."

"I'm not Santa," he grumbled as he went to the next bag.

She beamed and nodded before she went to untie the rest of the room.

One bag after the next they looked and looked, quietly calling, "Bo?"

Each child they freed joined the search.

Molly came running to Skip from another room. "I found him! I found a boy who says his name is Bo!"

Skip raced after her. Bo sat in a far room filled with scared kids and their now empty bags. His face was purple and puffy, and his eyes were swollen shut.

Skip knelt down before him and threw himself into his big brother's arms. They held each other quietly for a few moments, scared to move or let go.

"You gotta get out of here," Bo finally said, pushing Skip away. "He'll be back. You gotta get someplace safe."

The grownups outside had set off fireworks as the clock tower struck midnight.

"I am someplace safe," Skip replied.

Bo's swollen face smiled. He gently messed up Skip's hair.

"Guess what, Bo?" asked Skip. "You are on the nice list."

Skip reached into Santa's great big velvet sack. He

withdrew a single present wrapped in shiny red paper with a giant gold bow. "Merry Christmas."

Bo slowly took the present and unwrapped it. He became very quiet as he looked at his Christmas gift from Skip. "Markers."

"I told you Santa would bring you some. Now we can draw all day."

"I remember." He gave his brother a hug.

"Take that present back!" commanded a voice that rang with menace. "Your brother has been a very, very naughty boy."

Skip turned and looked over his shoulder. Standing there in the doorway was Krampus, his teeth barred and his hands upon his sack.

"I have the list, Krampus," said Skip, pulling out the piece of paper from his pocket and holding it up.

Krampus smiled. "Then you'll see what I say is true. All children are wicked. They will destroy you! They are hateful and ruin lives and no one wants them."

"That is a lie, Krampus!" Skip said.

"Lies all depend upon who is doing the telling."

Krampus threw down his sack and opened up the mouth.

"Don't move one more step, Krampus!" warned Skip.

"Or else what?"

"I said that I have the list!" said Skip, holding the paper even higher.

"And what of it?" asked Krampus. He pointed at the black bag on the ground and shouted, "You have disobeyed me! GET IN MY SACK YOU NAUGHTY BOY!"

The vortex emerged and it reached for Skip. It swirled around his legs and grabbed at his middle, but it couldn't pull him in. Instead, Skip seemed larger and stronger and much older than just eight. Power radiated from Skip's hand and his list began to glow with white heat.

Krampus shrank back with fear. Unbelieving, he whispered in a little voice, "Santa?"

Skip yelled, "I say who is naughty and nice! I have made the list! I have checked it twice! And do you recall who is the naughtiest creature of all?"

He held the list high with two hands, showing Krampus's name at top for all to see...

"You have been very, very naughty!" Skip shouted. He pointed at Krampus's velvet bag and yelled, "GET IN YOUR OWN SACK YOU NAUGHTY THING!"

Krampus began howling and clawing at the air. His hoofed feet slid upon the ground as if the floor was slicked with butter. He screamed as the wind picked him up and squeezed him, narrowing his body like meat through a grinder. It sucked him into the bag piece by piece until there was nothing left but silence.

And when he disappeared, the strangest thing began to happen. The noises outside changed. The revelry stopped and people were crying and calling out names.

"I'm here, Mom!" called one of the girls. The children all got up and ran towards the sound of their parents. Soon, the entire building was empty.

All except for that one little girl Skip had first freed. Molly stood there awkwardly alone, staring at the boys.

"What, kid?" asked Bo, roughly. "Don't you have some parents to go to or something?"

She shook her head. "No."

"It's okay, Bo. She helped," Skip walked over to her. "If I had a pen, I would put you on the 'nice' list, too."

She replied shyly, "Thanks."

"If you're on the nice list, that means I have to give you a present. What do you want for Christmas?" Skip asked.

Molly gulped. "I want to come with you and help make the toys..."

Her voice trailed off. Skip looked over at Bo and Bo shrugged. Skip replied carefully, "If that's your Christmas wish..."

She nodded.

Skip pointed above them. "The reindeer is on the roof."

The grin that spread across her face was slow, but it lit up the room before she raced off.

"Thank you, Santa!"

"I'm not..." but Skip couldn't finish the sentence.

Skip and Bo stood for a little while, the air around them echoing with laughter and tears and happy reunions.

"I'm scared, Bo," said Skip. He looked down at his suit and the paper he still clutched in his hands. "I think I have to be Santa Claus."

Bo didn't say anything for awhile. Then he shrugged and smiled. "You're good at it."

"What if someone like Krampus shows up again?"

Bo picked up Krampus's bag. "Well, I'll put them in this old sack and beat them with these sticks."

"I mean it."

"So do I." Bo looked at Skip and promised with every fiber of his being. "I'll come with you everywhere. I'll never let you out of my sight again. The worst was knowing I couldn't stop you from getting hurt. I'll always stay two steps behind, and no one will ever mess with you. I swear."

Skip leaned against Bo and gave him a hug. "I thought I'd never see you."

"Now you'll never get rid of me." Bo put Skip into a headlock and walked him to the door. "Come on, Skip. Let's catch that flying reindeer."

Skip laughed. He looked back at all the empty sacks littering the ground.

"How do you think someone like Krampus got to be so mean?" asked Skip.

With one hand filled with Krampus's bag and switch, Bo put his arm around his little brother. "I have no idea."

ABOUT THE AUTHOR

USA Today Bestselling author Kate Danley's debut novel The Woodcutter (47North) was honored with the Garcia Award for the Best Fiction Book of the Year, the 1st Place Fantasy Book in the Reader Views Literary Awards, and was the 1st place winner of the Sci-Fi/Fantasy category in the Next Generation Indie Book Awards. Her book *Queen Mab* was honored with the McDougall Previews Award for Best Fantasy Book. Her *Maggie MacKay: Magical Tracker* series has been optioned for film and television.

Her plays have been produced in New York, Los Angeles, and DC Metro area. She has over 300+ film, television, and theatre credits to her name, specializing in sketch, improv, and Shakespeare. She trained in on-camera puppetry with Mr. Snuffleupagus and played the head of a 20-foot dinosaur on an NBC pilot.

She lost on Hollywood Squares.

www.katedanley.com

ABOUT THE ILLUSTRATOR

Abigail Larson had ambitions of becoming an opera singer and joining the circus while growing up, and although neither of those ended up working out too well, she still enjoys both.

Abigail's work has been featured in many galleries across the United States and Europe, such as the Museum of American Illustrators in New York, The Poe Museum of Richmond, and Gallery Nucleus in California, and she has participated in many group gallery shows including Halloween Town's annual "Tribute to the Haunted Mansion" and Creature Features' "October Shadows" shows - not to mention prestigious venues in London, Paris, and Madrid.

Her work has been featured in various publications including *Spectrum Fantastic Art, Art Fundamentals,* and *Digital Artist* as well as several independent publishing houses. Her first fully illustrated children's book, *Sarah Faire and the House at the End of the World* written by Alex Giannini, was released in 2013.

www.abigaillarson.com

Made in the USA
Coppell, TX
13 March 2023

14188899R00030